IS IT TU B'SHEVAT YET?

CHRIS BARASH

Pictures by
ALESSANDRA
PSACHAROPULO

ALBERT WHITMAN & COMPANY
CHICAGO, ILLINOIS

When we look out the window
at trees dressed in browns

and smile to imagine their
leafy green gowns...

Tu B'Shevat is on its way.

When our cousins in Israel send pictures of bees

as they buzz around blooms on the pink almond trees...

Tu B'Shevat is on its way.

When Gran hurries in from
her trip to the store,

with dates, pomegranates, and olives galore...

Tu B'Shevat is on its way.

When Dad helps us make trees,
so crunchy and sweet,

from all kinds of nuts, fruits,
and seeds that we'll eat...

Tu B'Shevat is on its way.

When we work at the park and help spread the news
that we need to recycle, reduce, and reuse...

Tu B'Shevat is on its way.

When Mom's back from the nursery with seedlings in tow
and says we'll soon plant them and help them to grow...

Tu B'Shevat is on its way.

When our spades dig deep hollows as friends gather 'round,

and everyone helps place our trees in the ground...

When we reach out our hands as we happily say,

"Thank you, trees, for all that you give us each day!"

Tu B'Shevat is here!

Celebrate throughout the year with other books in this series!

To Matilde—AP

Library of Congress Cataloging-in-Publication data
is on file with the publisher.

Text copyright © 2019 by Chris Barash
Illustrations copyright © 2019 by Alessandra Psacharopulo
First published in the United States of America in 2019 by Albert Whitman & Company
ISBN 978-0-8075-6333-5 (hardcover)
ISBN 978-0-8075-6334-2 (ebook)

Printed in China
10 9 8 7 6 5 4 3 2 1 WKT 24 23 22 21 20 19
Design by Morgan Beck

For more information about Albert Whitman & Company,
visit our website at www.albertwhitman.com.

100 Years of Albert Whitman & Company
Celebrate with us in 2019!